Tips for Reading Together

Children learn best when reading is fun.

- Talk about the title and the pictures on the cover.
- Discuss what you think the story might be about.
- Read the story together, inviting your child to read as much of it as they can.
- Give lots of praise as your child reads, and help them when necessary.
- Try different ways of helping if they get stuck on a word. For example, get them to say the first sound of the word, or break it into chunks, or read the whole sentence again, trying to guess the word. Focus on the meaning.
- There are some tricky names in this Greek myth. For Midas say 'MY-dus'. For Dionysus say 'DY-oh-NY-sus'. For Olympus say 'o-LIM-pus'.
- Have fun finding the hidden fruit.
- Re-read the story later, encouraging your child to read as much of it as they can.

Children enjoy re-reading stories and this helps to build their confidence.

Have fun!

Find all the fruit hidden in the pictures.

The Golden Touch

Written by Roderick Hunt

Illustrated by Alex Brychta

OXFORD
UNIVERSITY PRESS

The children were dipping
strawberries into chocolate.
"They look yummy!" said Chip.
"They taste yummy!" said Kipper.

Kipper went to Biff's room. He had
chocolate on his hands. He got
chocolate on everything he touched.
"Go away, Kipper!" said Biff.

"You're getting chocolate on everything," said Chip.

"I wish everything I touched turned into chocolate," said Kipper.

"That's just greedy," said Chip.

Just then the magic key began to glow. It took the children into an adventure.

They saw a girl sitting by a river.

She was crying.

"What's the matter?" asked Biff.

"Come with me and I'll show you,"
said the girl. "My name is Zoe."
Zoe took them to a palace.

The children gasped. The palace
was made of gold, and a gold tree
stood outside.

Zoe took the children inside.
Everything was made of gold, even
the food on the table!

"My father is King Midas," said Zoe sadly. "He made a wish that everything he touched turned into gold. Now his wish has come true!"

"If the food turns into gold, how can he eat it?" asked Chip.

"He can't," said Zoe. "And if he touches me, I'll turn into gold too."

Just then King Midas came in.
Zoe hid behind Biff. "My father
used to hug me," she said, "but he
mustn't do it anymore."

King Midas saw Floppy. "I love
dogs," he said. "Come here!"

"Stop!" called Chip. "Don't touch that dog!"

It was too late. King Midas patted Floppy and he turned into gold.

"I'm so sorry," said King Midas.
"I forgot that everything I touch
turns into gold. I wish I could turn
him back into a real dog again."

"Who granted the wish?" asked Biff.

"It was Dionysus," said the king.

"Then we must go and see him," said Biff, "and ask him to help."

Dionysus lived on Mount Olympus.
It was a long way to walk, but at last
King Midas and the children arrived.

"Why have you come back to see me?" asked Dionysus.

"I have come to ask you to help me," said King Midas.

"I want everything back the way it was," said King Midas. "My wish was silly."

"You were foolish and greedy," said Dionysus. "But you have learnt your lesson. Now go back and do what I tell you."

Dionysus told them to get water from the river. They had to pour it onto everything that had turned into gold.

"It works!" said King Midas. "I'm
so glad your dog is back."
"So am I!" said Kipper.

King Midas gave Zoe a hug.
"What a fool I have been," he said.
"I'm glad I can hug you now. I will
never ask for gold again!"

King Midas looked at the children.
"Thank you for helping us," he said.

The key began to glow. It was
time to go home.

"Hey! Why did you do that?" asked Kipper, crossly.

"To stop you from turning into chocolate," laughed Chip.

Think about the story

Why was
Zoe crying?

How was
Floppy turned
into gold?

Why was
King Midas's wish
foolish and greedy?

What would
you wish for?

Matching pairs

Match each water carrier with his gold twin.

More books for you to enjoy

Level 1:
Getting Ready

Level 2:
Starting to Read

Level 3:
Becoming a Reader

Level 4:
Building Confidence

Level 5:
Reading with Confidence

OXFORD
UNIVERSITY PRESS

Great Clarendon Street,
Oxford OX2 6DP

Text © Roderick Hunt 2008
Illustrations © Alex Brychta 2008
This edition published 2010

First published 2008
All rights reserved

Read at Home Series Editors:
Kate Ruttle, Annemarie Young

British Library Cataloguing
in Publication Data available

ISBN: 9780198387701

10 9 8 7 6 5 4 3 2 1

Printed in China by Imago

Have more fun with Read at Home